For Mariam and all the incredible
women of Soufra.
—L. B.

To my grandma Sona. I still remember
all the dishes you made when visiting
us from Lebanon.
—S. A.

Library of Congress Cataloging-in-Publication Data available.

ISBN 978-1-7972-2233-2

Manufactured in China.

Design by Sandy Frank.
Typeset in Tiempos Text and Whitney.
The illustrations in this book were rendered digitally.

10 9 8 7 6 5 4 3 2 1

Chronicle books and gifts are available at special quantity
discounts to corporations, professional associations, literacy
programs, and other organizations. For details and discount
information, please contact our premiums department at
corporatesales@chroniclebooks.com or at 1-800-759-0190.

Chronicle Books LLC
680 Second Street
San Francisco, California 94107

Chronicle Books—we see things differently. Become part of
our community at www.chroniclekids.com.

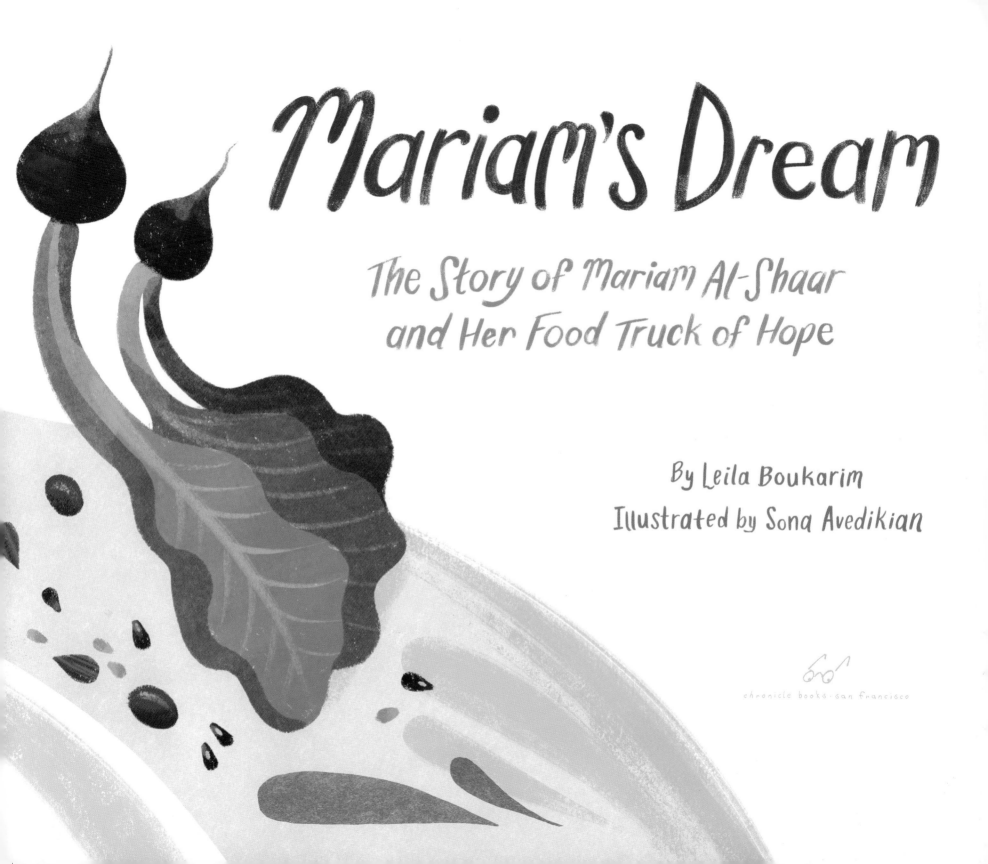

Mariam's Dream

The Story of Mariam Al-Shaar and Her Food Truck of Hope

By Leila Boukarim

Illustrated by Sona Avedikian

chronicle books·san francisco

In the heart of Beirut, the capital city of Lebanon, a refugee camp stirs, bursting at the seams.

Mariam was born here, but she will never be Lebanese.
She is Palestinian but may never go to Palestine.
Mariam is the daughter of refugees—
people who live between worlds.

Her whole life, Mariam has been surrounded by walls.

Walls that keep her from working,
from growing, from dreaming—
from being.

And Mariam has
always wanted more.

The streets of Mariam's camp brim with despair.

Men without work.

Children without schools.

Women without a say.

It's a familiar sight, the only one
Mariam has ever known.
But something deep inside her stirs.

Something tells her it doesn't have to be this way.
She wants to do something, and she knows she can't do it alone.
She doesn't have to do it alone.

Mariam reaches out to the women of her camp.
She wants to hear about their struggles, their ideas,
their dreams.

"What can we do?" she asks them.
"We want to cook," they tell her. "We are good at it."

Flavors from Palestine, Iraq, Syria, and Lebanon;
colors and scents of sumac, mint, cinnamon, and za'atar—
they have brought Mariam comfort and joy all her life.

It's settled.

Mariam puts together a kitchen.

She buys ingredients.

She makes lists and plans and phone calls.

And finally—

Soufra is born!

Soufra. A feast.
A table full of food.

A place where women get together to cook,
to sell their meals, and to earn a living.

But it's more than that.

It's where they go to share stories,
to laugh hard, and to be themselves.

Word travels fast around the camp. Women find the courage to step away from their duties at home and flock to Soufra—to Mariam—for a chance at something more.

Mariam watches her dream become a reality.
For the first time, she sees women choose what they want to do.

They have changed.
Their children have changed.
Mariam has changed.

It feels like her world is getting bigger.

There is so much more to explore. So much more to do.
So many more women to take in.

Mariam begins to make plans to take Soufra outside the camp walls, to reach more people and sell more food. Mariam dreams of a food truck!

But she will need money.
She will need to learn to drive.
She will need the right papers.

Some tell her it's impossible.
They tell her not to risk it.
But Mariam is determined.

People all around the world hear her story
and want to help. Mariam can hardly believe it.
Smiling from ear to ear, she picks out the perfect truck.

She can already imagine it carrying falafel
and mana'eesh, hummus and mousakhan.
She can't wait to begin.
But . . .

They tell her she can't own a truck.

She can't run a business outside her camp.
Her smile fades.

"I have all the papers you asked for. I have the money."

Speechless and heartbroken, she takes time to think.

And then she acts.
She makes phone calls
and writes letters
and tells her story to anyone who will listen.
She tells them about Soufra's delicious dolmas,
fragrant freekeh, and savory mansaf.

NO

after

NO

after

NO

are like bricks stacked high in a wall
that feels impossible to climb.

But she goes back to the kitchen where the women work hard and smile big. They are proud of the new role they play and of the fabulous food they make.

She can't stop now.

More walls stand in her way—
walls of rules,
of injustice,
of discrimination.
But Mariam has a mission.
She has a story.
She has a team of talented women who make food
that is meant to be shared.
No wall can stop her.
And so she charges ahead!

It takes two whole years . . .

But Mariam does it!

YES!

In the heart of Beirut, a refugee camp stirs,
bursting at the seams.

It is home to Mariam Al-Shaar,
her table full of food,
and refugees who dare to

dream of a better tomorrow.

"Every refugee has a dream, especially children.
They are always dreaming of a better life."

– Mariam Al-Shaar

Author's Note

Mariam Al-Shaar was born and raised in Bourj Al-Barajneh, an overcrowded refugee camp in Beirut, the capital city of Lebanon. Like many Palestinians, her parents were forced to leave Palestine in 1948. Although Mariam has lived her entire life in Lebanon, because of her refugee status, she is not allowed to do many of the things the citizens of Lebanon can.

I had the honor of interviewing Mariam in December 2018, after I had watched the documentary about her called *Soufra*. When I met her, I was incredibly moved by her quiet strength and remarkable modesty. I was touched by how much her community means to her. Mariam spoke mostly of the women who now make up her team. Soufra gave them a reason to leave the house, the courage to be who they are, and a chance to do what they love most— and get paid for it. Not only did these women grow happier and more confident, but they also inspired the children of the camp to dream of a better future. That, she said, is what Soufra really stands for.

Conditions at Mariam's refugee camp are difficult, particularly for women. But in the face of darkness and hopelessness, Mariam has dedicated herself to improving life there by empowering the people, by helping them learn the skills they need to do meaningful work. She is the kind of person who will do whatever it takes, for as long as it takes, to achieve her goals. She even learned to drive so that she could be the one to bring the food truck home. Since creating Soufra, Mariam has gone on to open a preschool as well as a Soufra Café in Bourj Al-Barajneh!

Today Soufra is known across Lebanon and around the world, with global visitors traveling all the way to Bourj Al-Barajneh just to meet the incredible woman who changed the lives of so many in her camp and inspired the children to dream big.

Food Glossary

The recipes for many of these dishes vary from country to country.

Dolma
Vine leaves stuffed with rice, meat, and tomatoes (called warak aareesh in Arabic)

Hummus
Dip made from chickpeas and tahini

Falafel
Deep-fried balls made from ground fava beans, chickpeas, or both

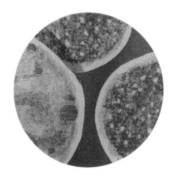

Mana'eesh
Flatbread topped with za'atar or cheese

Freekeh
Durum wheat served with chicken and roasted nuts

Mansaf
Lamb meat cooked in yogurt sauce and served with rice and roasted nuts

Mousakhan

Spiced roasted chicken served on flatbread with onions, pine nuts, and sumac

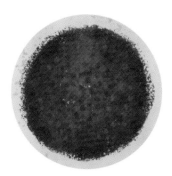

Sumac

A zesty red spice often used in Middle Eastern cooking

Za'atar

A mixture of oregano, marjoram, thyme, sesame seeds, and sumac, often mixed with lots of olive oil and eaten with pita or used to make mana'eesh

Refugees and Refugee Camps

A refugee is a person who is forced to leave their country to escape immediate danger, like war, climate disaster, political or religious persecution, or famine. A generational refugee is a person born to refugee parents who are not yet citizens of any country.

In 1948, 750,000 Palestinians were forced out of their homes in what is referred to as Al-Nakba, or *the catastrophe*. Of those, 110,000 ended up in refugee camps in neighboring Lebanon. These camps were set up as temporary accommodations, but years and decades have gone by, and refugee populations have grown to almost half a million. Tents have been replaced with concrete, but their infrastructure remains unsafe and unsanitary, sometimes resulting in illness and fatal accidents.

Although most Palestinians in Lebanon today were born and raised there, they are not granted the same rights as Lebanese citizens—most jobs are off-limits, and owning property is impossible, making the camps feel like prisons. And while they can technically move around the country as they please, most can't afford to leave their camps for good. Citizenship is not an option.

Currently the camps also house refugees from Syria, Iraq, and other countries, but the majority are still Palestinian. A refugee can be anyone and can come from anywhere. It's important to remember this and to understand that refugees are people who were displaced due to circumstances they could not control. No one wants to leave everything and everyone they know and love suddenly. But, tragically, these things happen. And when they do, it is up to the rest of us to help however we can: with a donation, a spare room, a meal, a kind word, or a smile and by speaking out against the injustices that led to their displacement. Every little bit counts.

At the time of this writing, there are over 100 million displaced people worldwide. To learn more about Palestinian refugees in Lebanon and how you can help, visit the United Nations Relief and Works Agency for Palestine Refugees in the Near East at unrwa.org.

Selected Bibliography

Al-Shaar, Mariam. Interview with the author. December 2018.

Morgan, Thomas, dir. *Soufra*. Charlotte, NC: Square Zero Films, 2017.

United Nations Relief and Works Agency for Palestine Refugees in the Near East. https://www.unrwa.org/.